THE ESSENCE OF LOVE

BY:
ANTHONY VAN MALONE SR.

Copyright © 2023 Anthony Van Malone, Sr.

Published by Dream2Life Publications Presents

All rights reserved.

No part of this book may be reproduced in any form without written consent of the publisher, except brief quotes used in reviews.

Acknowledgments

As always, I would like to give praise and honor to
GOD. Thank you for always
sustaining me throughout my life
and blessing me
with this awesome gift of poetry.
I thank you FATHER.
I would also like to thank my favorite teacher in the world,
Mrs. Meryl Dinowitz.
I was in her 7th grade class
when she told the class to write a poem
and I wrote my first poem right there
in her class,
and still to this day,
I am writing.
Thank you, my wonderful teacher
for pulling out my destiny.
To my family and friends,
thank you all for your

love and support.
Thank you to my Aunt Lou Lorraine Alexander
for always being there for everyone.
You always inspired
me to do better in life,
and I love you and thank you for your
love and inspiration throughout my life.
To my family,
you mean more to me than you
could ever imagine.
GOD truly blessed me with
an awesome family legacy
and my books will forever be in
our family archives
and I am very thankful for you all for
loving and forgiving me for so many mistakes
I made throughout my lifetime.
To my siblings, children, nephews, nieces, cousins,
grandchildren,
always do and be the best that you
can in this life and remember to put the Heavenly

Father first, always in your life.

Keep striving

at your best, even if it takes your last breath.

Thank you to Gerald Marcus family:

my grandpa and grandma

Roslie and Vincent Gerald,

the Malone family, Rita, Michele, Anthony Jr,

Jasmine, Jessica, Lakita, Elisa, Vincent,

Sheana Sinclair, and her dear mother and family.

You're always in my heart.

My sister Maryam Sani Mohammed and family,

Uncle Salu, Esha, Uncle Rabu, Rasheed,

Zurfau, Sada, Rabiatu, Aminatu.

Love you all.

Thanks for being the best family ever.

To my family:

Melvina Smiley, Hason Smiley, Joyel Smiley,

Amber Smiley, Mama and Papa Stevens,

Ma Marilyn Harris and family.

To Tamiko and the Edwards family.

To my brother Fred and the Woods family,

To my Aunt Katrina and cousin Sonia and the whole

Dewindt Family.

Special shoutout to my whole Universal Zulu Nation

brothers and sisters around the world.

Special shoutout to the Bronx divisions,

New York City section,

and my brother, my friend, Zulu King Native

Chapter 50 and Brother Scottie.

Shoutout to the South Bronx.

Shoutout to the Co-op City tennis club.

To my favorite neighbors on Desota Avenue in Cleveland

Heights, Tony and Annette,

Joe, Gregg, my nephew James AKA Bear Mike, Ethan, Kai,

Demeiro, my son Devon, and Renee Boss from the Bronx.

Marcus, Curtis, and Gregg, my Desota family.

Shout out to my people:

cousin Jessie and his family,

my cousin Kelli and her family,

my dear friends from Ohio,

Tiffany and her family.

To my dear friend from Walton High School,

Brenda Vargas and her family.

To my family I lost that will always be in my

memory and heart forever,

my dearest grandma and grandpa,

Roslie and Vincent Gerald.

Thank you so much for my West Indian roots.

To my dearest mother,

Patricia Emily Malone. R.I.P.

To my dearest uncle Darriel Antonio Felix.

I can still hear your drums in my head. R.I.P.

To my dearest uncle Milton,

I still hear your voice singing in my ear.

Thanks for those talks and fond memories.

To my dearest Sani Mohammed.

Thank you for being that dad I never had

and always being there to set me straight when I went astray. R.I.P.

To dearest Uncle Ace,

Thank you for so much.

You were truly there from the beginning to the end,

and words cannot express how I really feel.

So R.I.P.

R.I.P. Cousin Ziggy

R.I.P. cousin Keith Jones

R.I.P. to cousin Chynna Dewindt

R.I.P. to my nephew Weegee.

R.I.P. to Mama Betty,

R.I.P. to my brother-in-law,

Anthony Garcia AKA Savage.

R.I.P. to Leroy Smiley.

R.I.P. Tonia Michelle Velez.

R. I. P. to my pets, Zack and Zo'ie.

Dedication:

I'd like to dedicate this book to

my mother and my grandparents

for always instilling in me morals and love

and implanting in me the fear of the Most High, GOD

and to my publisher, my friend, my fiancée and lover

Sherene Holly

and the Stephens Family.

Thank you for turning my dreams 2 life.

If I have forgotten anyone,

please know that you are in my

heart and thoughts

and I will definitely remember you.

Book #2 is coming.

TABLE OF CONTENTS

(1) A BLACK MAN'S TEARS FOR HIS PEOPLE

(2) CALL FOR HELP

(3) ALWAYS

(4) ALL IN ONE BREATH

(5) ALL YOU NEED IS TIME

(6) AMAZING LOVE

(7) A PROMISE TO MY WIFE

(8) A QUESTION OF GUILT

(9) A THANKSGIVING STORY DEDICATED TO MAMMA

(10) BEAUTIFUL BLACK WOMEN

(11) BEAUTIFUL FACES

(12) BLACK LOVE

(13) BRENDA

(14) BROWN EYES

(15) BURRY ME HERE

(16) CONJOINED HEARTS

(17) CRACK

(18) DEAR FRIEND OF MINE

(19) DEAR GOD

(20) DEAR LORD

(21) DO YOU REMEMBER

(22) DREAMING OF YOU (23) ENOUGH

(24) EVEN THOUGH I NEVER SEEN YOU

(25) ACCEPT GOD'S HOLY SPIRIT

(26) FAITH

(27) FAREWELL FOR NOW

(28) FEELINGS

(29) FEELINGS OF LOVE

(30) FOR THOSE WHO KNEW ME

(31) FRIENDS FOREVER

(32) GET YOUR HOUSE IN ORDER

(33) GIRLS ARE SEXY

(34) GOD SAID

(35) GOD SENT ME AN ANGEL

(36) GONE BUT NOT FORGOTTEN

(37) HAVE I FOUND YOU

(38) HAVE YOU EVER

(39) HELL BEGIN'S

(40) HOW

(41) HOW BEAUTIFUL OUR GOD IS
(42) HOW BEAUTIFUL YOU ARE TO ME

(43) HOW MANY HEARTACHES

(44) I AM FALLING IN LOVE

(45) I AM FOREVER IN LOVE WITH YOU

(46) I AM GOING TO MISS YOU

(47) I AM ME

(48) I AM SO DEPRESSED WITHOUT YOU

(49) I AM SO LONELY

(50) I AM SO LONELY WITHOUT YOU

(51) WHERE IAM FROM

(52) OUR LOVE

(53) OUR BLACKNESS IS BEAUTIFUL AND POWERFUL

(54) A PLAN TO ERADICATE THE BLACK RACE

(55) ALL I EVER WANTED

A BLACK MAN'S TEARS FOR HIS PEOPLE

We're living

mainstream,

destroying

each other's

dreams

by not

understanding

who we are

as black people!

Not opening

our eyes

to really see

that we're

destroying

our future.

Not!

The white man's

his story!

We're hanging

ourselves

on our own

limb tree!

With no

education,

structure

or

ability!

Our black people

are using guns

in place

of a

lynching tree!

We might

as well

put a rope

around

our brother's

neck

to hang!

It's better

To get away

with murder

with a quiet

sound of a rope

than a sound

of a shotgun!

Blast!

With a bang.

We complain

that our families

are no longer

connected

anymore.

We are,

just look

inside

the prisons!

Our black faces,

and

families

ae spread out

Wall

to

wall.

Nothing has changed

We're no different

than those

white men

who tried

to destroy

our race

back then!

Same objective,

Different style,

different face!

Our own

black men,

are destroying us

from the face

of the earth!

We're now

killing off

the black Race,

Now!

our colors

are no longer

proudly worn

in the pigment

of our

face and skin,

now the proudness

comes from

a rag

in our pockets

within!

Before

it was white men

riding horses!

Wearing hoods,

Now!!

It's

Low riders,

black faces,

in our own

hood!

Committing

genocide,

Acts of

homicide,

generation

suicide...

A CALL FOR HELP

She was alone

And she could see a shadow.

So, she tried to run

But she could not see

Where was she running.

She was trapped

And there was nothing

She could do.

She screamed

and called for help

But no one could hear her.

What was she doing

In that dark place?

Was she taking a short cut?

We will never know

We just won't know...

ALWAYS

Always

You take my heart away,

You have my heart

In your hands,

Your touch

Is never enough,

For me.

Your eyes,

Always in a day,

Through heaven,

I see,

You're an angel,

Always

Sent from above,

For me,

Through the word of GOD

I truly believe,

When he said,

He will sustain me,

And fulfill all of my needs,

He blessed me,

And gave you,

To me,

You're all

my dreams,

My destiny,

For my lifetime,

You're my ultimate,

Love fantasy

To You

my wife:

You're everything!

I

Ever wanted,

You're everything

I ever dreamed

of

The way love

Should be....

I dedicate this poem

Because you,

Love me,

The way love

Should be.

I love you dearly

Dedicated to my wife:

I will always love you.

ALL IN ONE BREATH

We laugh

We cry

We see

We're blind

We touch

We feel

We give life

We kill

We see what's fake

And understand

What's real

We're complexed

And yet

We're amused

We're intelligent

But many

Are fools

We're evil

We're good

If

We could

We would

We love

We hate

We give

We take

We open

We close

We're young

We're old

We're weak

We're strong

We're hot

We're cold

We're right

We're wrong

We stop

We go

We know

And then again

We Don't

We're above

We're below

We're flesh

We're dust

We enter

We exit

And put

To our death!

All in one breath.

All YOU NEED IS TIME

All you need is time

To make up your mind

Because I already

Made up mine

It's you who I want

To have

and to hold

But if you're not sure

You want me

Don't let me suffer

Tell me

And let me go

Who is it going to be

Me or your guy

Who's far away

And never near

Who's gone

But look around

Because I am still here

Time is all you need

To make up your mind

You don't know if you

Lost your boyfriend

But it's better to lose one

Than two at the same time

Please open your eyes

And see

Is it him

Or

Is it me

After all the things

That we've been through

My love is still

Going strong

For you

We've been having

This sweet love a fare

But it's time to wake up

And see who really cares

I know that things

Always Change

But this love

I have for you

Will always

stay the same

So, take my love

Wherever

your heart

Shall dwell

And

just remember

Without a fight

I will never

Let you go.

AMAZING LOVE

I LOVE YOU!

LISTEN

TO MY WORDS

OF A MAN

THAT

LOVES YOU.

I LOVE YOU!

PUT YOUR HEART

INTO MY HANDS

AND LET ME

SHOW YOU

WHAT LOVE

IS ALL ABOUT.

LET ME BE

YOUR POETRY,

LET ME BE

ALL

OF THE WORDS

YOU'LL EVER NEED

IN ME,

LET ME BE

THAT SECURITY.

LET ME

SO LOVE

YOUR HEART

AND

BE

YOUR HEART'S

DESTINY.

LET ME

TAKE YOU

TO ECSTASY

WITH MY LOVE,

LET ME

SHOW YOU

AND

TELL YOU

THINGS

YOU'VE NEVER

KNOWN.

LET MY

GODLY LOVE

BE THE ANSWERS

TO YOU

AND

YOUR PRAYERS

FOREVER,

LET ME

BE

THAT MAN,

THAT FRIEND,

THAT HUSBAND,

THAT LOVER,

FALL IN ALL

THAT YOU NEED

AND

WANT

ME TO SAY

AND

DO.

LET ME

BE

THAT FANTASY,

THAT THOUGHT,

THOSE WISHES,

THOSE PRAYERS!

IN ALL,

LET ME

BE

THAT GODLY

DREAM

COME TRUE.

LET ME

PUT YOU

TO SLEEP

WITH JUST

MY GENTLE WORDS,

LET ME

SERENADE

YOUR HEART,

LET ME

CARESS

YOUR HEART,

LET ME

FINESS

YOUR HEART.

I WANT TO FEEL

THE RHYTHM

OF

YOUR HEARTBEAT

AGAINST MINE
I WANT TO FEEL
YOUR SOFT,
SWEET,
SILKY HAIR.
I WANT
YOUR TONGUE
AND
MY TONGUE
TO HAVE
THEIR SWEET
CONVERSATION
TOGETHER,
NOT FOR JUST
A MOMENT
BUT
FOR ALWAYS
AND FOREVER.
I DREAM
OF ALL
THESE THINGS
THAT I WANT
TO DO

TO YOU

AND

WITH YOU,

I WANT

TO FEEL

THE TOUCH

OF YOUR HANDS

AGAINST MY CHEST.

I WANT

TO WHISPER

THAT

I LOVE YOU

IN YOUR EAR

I WANT

TO HOLD YOU

SO GENTLE

AND

OH

SO CLOSE,

I WANT

TO SMELL

YOUR

SILHOUETTE,

A SMELL

THAT

I KNOW

I WOULD

NEVER

FORGET

I WANT

TO TASTE

YOUR LIPS

ON MINE

NO NEED

TO RUSH,

LETS TAKE

OUR TIME.

I WANT

TO HEAR

THE BEAT

OF YOUR HEART,

TO COUNT

THE EVERY

SKIP

OF MINE.

I WANT

TO FEEL

YOUR GENTLENESS

I WANT YOU

TO FEEL

EVERY INCH,

OF ME

I WANT TO

TASTE

EVERY TASTE

Of YOUR JUICY

WET

SUCCULENT

BODY.

I WANT

TO WIPE

THE TEARS

OF

YOUR JOY

AND

HAPPINESS

WITH MY

FINGER TIPS

AS I MAKE

YOUR BODY

SHAKE,

QUIVER,

AND

EXPLODE

WITH MY LOVE.

THESE

ARE ALL

OF

THE THINGS

THAT

I WANT

TO DO

TO YOU,

FOR YOU,

FOR ME

BECAUSE

I LOVE YOU

SO DEEPLY

SO MUCH

BECAUSE

I AM TOUCHED.

A PROMISE TO MY WIFE

I promise to be there

For you,

In everything you do

I promise to be truthful

And faithful

Just for you

I promise to learn from you,

In everything,

That

you want to teach

And

I promise

That only soft

Sweet words

Will be spoken,

Every time

that I speak,

I promise

to hold You

and

comfort You

in every kind of

Way,

I promise to cherish you,

And

protect you,

Each

And

Every,

Single day,

I promise to change

For you,

To become a better man,

Just be patient with me,

And I will show you,

That I can,

I promise to curve

my rough edges

And to change my attitude,

To a meek

and

humble one,

Like Christ,

I promise

to

live my life,

By bible base standards,

If you become my wife,

I promise to fulfill,

All your

Needs

Wants

And

cares,

And

to always

Be there,

To wipe

away your tears,

I promise

to communicate,

With you

And

give you my heart,

And

never

keep

anything inside,

That will keep us

apart,

I promise

these things,

For you,

Because

I love you,

So much,

I promise

to change,

Because

It's your heart,

I forever want,

To touch!

You are my

Best friend

You are my

Wife,

You are my

Whole

world,

And

the love

of my

Life...

A QUESTION OF GUILT

A question of guilt

The people had to say

A question of guilt

And he would

be sent away

Away

to be doomed

Away

to be lost

A question of guilt

And

that

was the cause...

A THANKSGIVING STORY

A THANKSGIVING

DEDICATED TO MAMA

We were so poor

We wore each other's clothes

We were so poor

We used brown paper bags

to blow Our nose

Mama

barely made enough money

but we always seem

to get by,

Because the more money

Mama would make

the more prices

would get high!

We had food

but it would only last

Until the end of the week,

we couldn't wait

until Thanksgiving

because that would be the day

we really got to eat

We didn't have turkey

like everyone else

because the price

of turkey was so high,

so we settled

for canned beef

and

Bread bean pie

that Mama made

Herself.

She had to use

a lot of Ingredients

that she couldn't afford

to buy

We would ask her

where she would get it

we would ask her

if she made it herself,

and she would tell us
that she found it

on the supermarket shelf.

We would then believe

that GOD did work

in mysterious ways,

because Mama seem

to find things

Come Those very special days

we always seemed to pray

and wish

that things got better

for us

and it did

as we got older

we never forgot

how Mama loved us

so much,

Mama's gone now!

GOD rest her soul

she looked so young

when she had died

but I guess her age

had told her

that it was time for her

to go.

Well,

as we gather around

and look

at our Thanksgiving table

at the things we didn't have

then

like turkey, yams,

fresh bread,

and red royal jelly.

We all thank GOD

that we have this now

to fill our humble bellies

as we all bend our heads

to pray

and thank GOD

that everyone is here

except Mama

sharing this

Thanksgiving day.

Dear Lord,

Bless Mama

Wherever she's at

And tell her

Dear LORD

That we will never

forget

How she loved us,

fed us

and

tried

To get us fat

We also thank

GOD

For the things

we didn't Have

and the things we

Now got,

we thank you

GOD

really

For all of that.

Dedicated to my beloved mama

Rest in peace dear heart...

BEAUTIFUL BLACK WOMEN

My beautiful black women

With your fascinating

Hair,

Nails,

And feet

You have your A game together

Ready to compete

No one can stop you

Or even compare

Before words are even spoken

You let us know

Not to go there

My beautiful black women

So strong

But yet

So vain,

Give true brothers

A Chance

And stop playing

These games.

You say

You need a real man

But we can't

Even get to your heart,

Before we start talking

You start tearing us apart.

It shouldn't be about

Our clothes

Or materialistic things,

What it should be about

Is what we can do

For you

Through the essence

That we bring.

Like the warmth

In our hearts

And the silk

In our touch

And the words

That we speak

That articulates

Us.

These are the things

That you should look for

In a man

And love

So very much,

So give us a chance

To express

What we feel

Let us show you

That our hearts

Are genuine

And our love

Is really

Real...

BEAUTIFUL FACES

I see beautiful faces

Wherever I go

They're beautiful to me

Even though

If

They don't know

I see beauty in their eyes

Even when

They are closed

I see beauty in their color

Their lips

And

their nose

I see beauty in their smiles

When it captures the world

I see beauty in these women

And

phenomenal girls

I see beauty

When they think

That they are

all alone

And

no one

is looking

I see beauty

From my eyes

From the pictures

That has

Been taken

I see beauty

In their silence

Without an utter word spoken

It's beauty to me

They don't have to say

Nothing

I see beauty in all women

They all have their part

On those beautiful faces

That reflects

Through

Their Hearts.

BLACK LOVE

OUR STYLE

AND

GRACE ARE UNIQUE

AND

MY MANHOOD

IS TRUE

IT'S AS BIG

AS MY FEET,

AND

YOUR STYLE

AND

WAYS

ARE

LIKE SILK,

SO SMOOTH

AND

SO SLEEK!

AND

WHEN YOU

PUT IT DOWN

ON ME,

IT'S WORDS

I CAN

NOT FIND

TO SPEAK!

YOUR BODY

YOUR BREASTS

ARE

SO SOFT

SO SWEET

SO RIPE

SO RIGHT

AND YOUR

MOIST

SUCCULENT

VAGINA

WHEN IAM IN YOU

OOH

I FEEL SO GOOD

SO WET

OOH

SO DAMN TIGHT!

BLACK

IS BEAUTIFUL

BUT

BLACK

LOVE

IS SO

MUCH

MORE!

PUMPING, SWEATING,

GRINDING

SO HARD

AS OUR

SWEAT

HITS

GLOWS

AND

GLISTENS

THE

FLOOR,

AS YOU'RE

NIBBLING

ON

MY BODY

AND

SCREAMING

MORE

I WANT

MORE!

AS YOU

REACH

YOUR

CLIMAX

FOR

HIGHER

HEIGHTS

TO SORE,

AS I

HOLD ON

TIGHT

TO YOU

AND

YOU

HOLD ON

TIGHT

TO ME,

AS

I

PINCH,

SQUEEZE

AND

SMACK

YOUR

ASS

YES,

YOUR

PHAT BOOTY

SO SWEET

AND

TENDERLY!

GIRL,

YOU GOT BACK!

MOST DEFINITELY!

BLACK LOVE IS YOU!

IT'S PASSION

IT'S DESIRE

IT'S YOUR

HEART

AND

SOUL

I

ADMIRE,

AND
WANT
SO
MUCH
MORE
YOU'RE
A
GODDESS,
YOU'RE
ONE
OF
A
KIND
YOU'RE
MY
BEAUTIFUL
MAGNIFICENT
QUEEN
OF ALL
TIMES.
NO ONE
CAN EVER
TAKE YOUR PLACE

OR

PLAY YOUR ROLE,

BECAUSE

YOU ARE

APART OF ME

MY BLACKNESS

MY LOVE,

MY LIFE,

MY LIVING

BLACK SOUL.

DEDICATED TO BLACK LOVE.

BRENDA

That B is for your beauty

That is captured in your smile,

The R is for remembering

How much you make my life

Worth its while.

The E is for my emptiness

My heart feels

When you're never around,

The N is for me needing you

And needing you right now,

For only you

Can fulfill my smile.

The D is for my dream came true

When we first met,

The A is for I'll always and Forever

Remember you,

Because you're very special

And special people like yourself

Is so very hard

To forget.

Dedicated to my High School friend,

Brenda Vargas.

BROWN EYES

I can see a whole world

In your eyes

A world

filled with care

And

in this world

I see me there,

In this world

I see in your eyes

I see happiness

And wishes

By looking

in your eyes

Makes me

want to be with you

Forever

And share your tender kisses

In this world

I see

In everything you touch

The reason why I feel this way

Is because

I love you

So much...

BURY ME HERE

BURY ME HERE

IT'S TIME

FOR ME

TO LEAVE

AND

I KNOW

IT'S NOT

FAIR

BUT IT'S

TIME FOR ME

TO GO

I HAD

NO CHOICE

SO

BURY ME HERE

NEXT TO MY MOTHER

IT'S WHERE I WANT TO BE

WHETHER ABOVE

OR BELOW,

I AM STILL

WITH FAMILY!

I TRAVELED A LONG ROAD

I MADE SO MANY MISTAKES

AND TRIED

SO MANY TIMES

TO CORRECT THEM

ALONG THE WAY

AND ONLY

ACCEPTING THE LORD'S

SALVATION!

AGREED WITH MY STAY,

AND MY PRAYERS

TO GOD ABOVE

KEPT ME ALIVE

EACH AND EVERY

DAY,

MY LIFE

WAS NOT EASY

I TOOK

THE BUMPS

AND

THE BRUISES

AND

KEPT ON GOING!

BEFORE THE LORD'S SALVATION

I WAS LIVING A CRUCIAL LIFE

ON MY OWN!

HEADING

FOR SOMETHING

BUT REALLY

NEVER KNOWING!

I AM TIRED NOW

IT'S TIME FOR ME

TO REST.

I DID

WHAT I HAD

TO DO

IN THIS

LIFETIME,

I TRIED

MY HARDEST

TO GET

THINGS RIGHT

I THINK

I DID

MY VERY BEST

I MADE FRIENDS

I MADE ENEMIES

ALL ALONG

THE WAY,

IT DOESN'T

MATTER

WHAT PEOPLE

THINK

IT DOESN'T MATTER

WHAT PEOPLE

SAY

BECAUSE

I WILL BE

GONE!

IN MY LOW

AND

RESTING PLACE!

AND

I WOULDN'T

BE ABLE TO HEAR

THEM ANYWAY.

SOME WILL

LAUGH,

SOME WILL

CRY

SOME WILL

BE HAPPY,

SOME WILL

BE BENT

SOME WILL

BE BROKEN

AND

SOME

WILL DIE

INSIDE!

BUT IF YOU

MUST

REMEMBER

ME,

REMEMBER

THAT I WAS

ONE OF A KIND

SWEET

AND

A GENTLE

KIND OF MAN

WHO DID

WHATEVER

AND

WHENEVER

I COULD

WHENEVER

I CAN!

SOME

WILL ONLY

REMEMBER ME

FOR THE INTIMATE

MOMENTS

THAT WE SHARED.

SOME

WILL CRY HARD

AND

OTHERS WILL

WEEP

BUT

SOME

IN THEIR HEARTS

THEY WON'T

REALLY CARE

THAT

I'M GONE,

I'M DEAD,

I'M RESTING

I'M ENJOYING

MY ETERNAL

SLEEP.

SO,

BURY ME HERE

THIS IS

AS GOOD

AS ANY,

AND

IF

YOU'RE WONDERING

IF

I AM GETTING

MY REST,

MY SLEEP.

DON'T WORRY,

TRUST ME

I AM IN

GOD'S HANDS

I AM IN

GOD'S CARE!

AND YES

I AM GETTING

PLENTY!

SO AFTER

THE ASHES

TO ASHES

AND

THE DUST

TO DUST,

NEVER

FORGET ME

FAMILY

NEVER

FORGET ME

FRIENDS

IN YOUR HEARTS.

BUT FOR NOW

TURN AWAY,

WALK AWAY

AND

GO

LIVE IT UP!

BUT NEVER

FORGET

WHERE YOU

BURIED ME!

CONJOINED HEARTS

TRUE LOVE

IT ESSENTIALLY MEANS

SOMEONE

WHO HAS BECOME

FAR MORE IMPORTANT

THAN YOURSELF

AND YES

I AM IN LOVE

WITH YOU

BECAUSE OF THE THINGS

THAT I WOULD RATHER DO

FOR YOU

THAN FOR

MYSELF

YOU ARE

THE ONE

THAT I

CARE FOR

YOU ARE

THE ONE

THAT I

THINK ABOUT

EACH

AND

EVERY DAY

YOU ARE

LOCKED

FOREVER

IN MY HEART

AND

COULD NEVER

FADE AWAY

LOVE

IT'S AN

ENDURING QUALITY

WITHIN

FALLING DEEPLY,

WHOLEHEARTEDLY

IN LOVE

EVERY THOUGHT

THAT YOU

THINK ABOUT

EVERY SECOND

THAT YOU SPEND

I'M ABOUT YOU

OVER

AND

OVER

AGAIN

AND

AGAIN

WE ARE

CONJOINING HEARTS

STUCK

BY LOVE

JOINED TOGETHER

BY

GOD

IT STAYS

WITH YOU

IT'S GENUINE

IT'S DIFFERENT

IT'S HONEST

IT'S NEW

THERE'S ONLY ROOM

FOR ONLY ME

THERE'S ONLY ROOM

FOR ONLY YOU

JOINED TOGETHER

BY GOD

THAT MAKES IT

SO TRUE

I LOVE YOU

I LOVE YOU

LIKE

I'VE NEVER

LOVED

ANYONE ELSE

I LOVE YOU

SO MUCH

MORE

IN SPITE OF

MYSELF

WE ARE SUSPENDED

IN TIME

WHILE

THE WHOLE WORLD

SEEMS

SO STILL

WITH

FOND MEMORIES

AND

DAY-BY-DAY

OCCURRENCES

IS HOW

YOU MAKE ME FEEL

TRUE LOVE

IT FEEDS YOU

MORE

THAN ANY

NOURISHMENTS

YES

YOU FEEL FULL

IN THE PRESENCE

OF LOVE

YET

YOU KNOW

IT'S NOT

FULLY PHYSICAL

BUT

MORE SPIRITUAL

FROM GOD

THE TREATMENT

OF LOVE

CAN NEVER

BE CURED

BECAUSE

WE KNOW

THAT WE

ARE JOINED

TOGETHER

FROM GOD

ABOVE

WE ARE ONE

EXTREMELY

SPIRITUALLY

CONNECTED

ENDURING

GOD'S LOVE

JOINED

AND

FASTENED

FOREVER

IT IS

WHAT KEEPS

US TOGETHER

WE CAN'T EVER

BE SEPARATED

OR

SEVERED APART

BECAUSE

IT'S A SPIRITUAL

BOND

THAT KEEPS US

TOGETHER,

DEEP DOWN

IN OUR

HEARTS.

Crack

There's a new drug in town

Called crack

And it's gotten around.

Crack,

It's a deadly new form of cocaine,

One puff out of this

And it destroys the brain.

How can we stop

Our children from taking,

They want to have fun?

But not this

They're mistaken,

Crack

How widely it is used

Can only be guessed,

But it's best results

Are horrifying

Addiction and death.

Crack

Its cost is so little

School children can find

Enough change in their pockets

For a nickel or dime.

And

if

they can't

find

it

More

Quicker

than others,

Their first

Prerogative

Is to Rob

Or

murder

Our

Sisters,

Our

Brothers.

Dear friend of mine

Dear friend of mine

I have to say,

It's time

We separate

And go

The opposite way.

We've come

To the end

of the road

It's been long,

It's been hard.

And now

One of us

Must go

For we have shed

So many tears

And been through

So many years.

I can remember

Years of pain

And years

Of laughter,

So many years

We shared

Forever after.

And

Because of this

I'll remember you

Till the day

I die

Always,

Dear friend of mine...

DEAR GOD

DEAR GOD,

Walk with me

Talk with me

Shine on me

divinely

Take my hand

And set me free

Come into my heart

And show me

The way

It should be

DEAR GOD,

Up above

Full of grace

Filled with love

Hold me

Guide me

Set yourself

Beside me

Watch me

Protect me

As I lay

And as

I sleep

As I laugh

And as I cry

Never leave

By my side

You're

my GOD

I praise You

High!

Without you,

I would die.

Dear Lord

Dear Lord,

Guide me through

My daily task

Guide me through

Darkness

By

holding my hands

Guide me through

Fire

water

And

smoke

And

if I sin

Let me repent

Don't let me choke

For I am the one

You call your son

There are millions

of us

But I am

The voice

Of just

Only one

I thank thee

Lord

For your mercy

And love

I thank thee

Lord

From the heavens

Above.

Do you remember

Do you remember

When we first

Laid eyes

On each other?

I do

And I felt then

As I do now

I could no longer

Look at another

Do you remember

When we first

said hello?

I do

And right there

And then

I knew

that

I would

Never let you go.

Do you remember

When we first

Walked

Side by side?

I do

And I thought then

As I still think now

That without you

By my side,

I would just

Die!

If I could no longer

Look into

Your soft

Beautiful

Brown eyes!

Do you remember

When I first

Laid your hands

Into mine?

I do

We were both

Trembling

But we did not

Question

Because deep down

Inside,

We both

Knew why.

Do you remember

Our first kiss?

I do

And

I'll never

Forget you

Nor your

Sweet

And

tender

Lips.

DREAMING OF YOU

While I awoke

Upon my dreams

I looked around

to where

you ought to be

And realized

that you were not

by my side

And that makes me

wonder

how I get through

the night

as I toss and turn

in a raging fit

as I awoke

from my dream

it's you

who I missed

with tears

in my eyes

and worry

in my heart

I don't know

how much longer

you and I

could be apart

we were making love

and your hands

were in mine

I was giving it

to you

nice and slow

because I thought

I had time

as you rode me

like a pony

more than ten times

over and over

again and again

steeper than deeper

as long as you

were on me

and I

was in you

you were mine

As though

it may seem

because as soon

as you got off me

you disappeared

and I exploded

soaked and wet

all over my bed

damn!

not again

you were

just another dream

just another memory

stuck in my head

with thoughts

Of you

On my mind.

ENOUGH

Enough

With the hatred

Enough

With the lies

Enough

With the attitudes

And the rolling

Of the eyes

Enough

With the bickering

The fighting

And the fuss

Enough

With the meanness

The acting so tough

We need to rise up

And stop killing

Our own

That's enough

Raising our children

In the streets

We need to go back

To the basics

And raise our children

Back in our homes

Where we

taught them

How

To love

To live

To care

To give

And

to understand

That we have to

Respect each other

And welcome

With open arms

Our sisters

Our brothers

Let us raise our children

The way

GOD

Intended

GOD

Gave us

A free eternal gift

So let's not

throw it away

So let's not

Spend it

Enough

With the abuse

Enough

With the pain

Enough

With the coarse words

Where there's

Nothing to gain

Let's build our lives

On the word of GOD

If we take that road

And trust in Him

Our lives won't be

So hard

Enough

Is

Enough.

EVEN THOUGH I NEVER SEEN YOU

Even though

I've never seen you

You're exquisite,

My heart has seen you,

Many times,

And in my heart,

You belong to me,

Yes!

You are mine,

You're exotic in a way,

I have never seen

My eyes have held

Some beauty before,

But you,

My heart adores.

Your silhouette is a smell

I could never regret,

When my heart

made love

To you,

It was such

a sweet

Savory smell

I could never forget.

But yet

I can't explain it

Because it doesn't exist,

It was just my heart's

Imagination

Of your perfume mist.

Even though

I have never

heard your voice,

In my heart,

I have heard you

Many times,

As your soft, sweet whispers

Ministers to my heart

About your love

for me,

As you take me

to the height

Of your ecstasy.

You intoxicate my heart

With your love,

And it's

the sweetest wine

My heart has ever

Tasted.

Even though

I have never tasted your lips,

My heart

Has tasted your lips

To a satisfying degree,

That lets me know

That your love belongs to me.

Even though

I have never

touched you,

My heart

Has touched you

In many ways

That makes me quiver,

And tremble,

And makes you

Have Orgasms

Days.

After.

Days.

After.

Days.

Your heart

And

my heart

Has an intimacy

Together

You excite me

In more ways

Than you know,

My heart,

Is so in touch

by you

And

it just wants

To hold you,

And never,

Let you go.

ACCEPT GOD'S HOLY SPIRIT

WHEN WE ACCEPT

GOD'S HOLY SPIRIT

WE ALLOW GOD

TO GUIDE US

THROUGH

HIS HOLY SPIRIT

WE SEE EXACTLY

WHAT GOD

WANTS

US TO SEE

THROUGH

HIS SPIRITUAL EYES

SO THAT WE HAVE A BETTER

UNDERSTANDING OF HIMSELF!

THIS IS THE LEVEL

THAT GOD WANTS

ALL OF US

TO BE ON!

WHEN WE

ACCEPT THE GIFT

OF SPIRITUAL

GUIDANCE

AND

SPIRITUAL SIGHT!

IT IS THE ONLY WAY

THAT WE CAN SEE GOD!

AND TRULY

UNDERSTAND HIS LOVE,

PLAN AND PURPOSE

FOR US

IN OUR LIVES!

BUT WE HAVE TO

WHOLEHEARTEDLY

SUBMIT TO HIS WILL

HOLDING NOTHING BACK,

AND TRUSTING IN GOD,

AND RELEASING

OUR PHYSICAL ENTITIES!

AND

HAVING FAITH

IN GOD'S SPIRITUAL ENTITIES,

FOR THINGS

THAT ARE NOT SEEN

THAT

FROM GOD!

WE HOLD STRONG

IN BELIEFS AND FAITH!

AND FOR US,

IT IS COUNTED

AS RIGHTEOUS.

FOR WE KNOW

IN OUR HEARTS

THAT THESE

ARE THE THINGS,

THAT COMES FROM

OUR MERCIFUL,

JUST!

AND

RIGHTEOUS

FATHER

TRUST AND BELIEVE!

AND STAND STRONG

IN SPIRIT

AND

FAITH

AND YOU SHALL NOT

BE MOVED!

FOR NO ONE

CAN TAKE ANYTHING

OUT OF

GOD'S HANDS!

WHEN YOU BELONG

TO HIM.

INSPIRED BY: GOD

KING JAMES BIBLE:

ROMANS: 4-5 BUT TO HIM THAT WORKETH NOT, BUT BELIEVETH ON HIM THAT JUSTFIETH THE UNGODLY, HIS FAITH IS COUNTED FOR RIGHTEOUSNESS...

FAITH

Believe in this word

Believe in me.

Believe in what I write

Believe in what I say,

And the joy of faith

Will shine your way.

Believe in yourself

Believe in what you do,

And the happiness of faith

Will always be with you.

Believe in what you are

Believe in what you have done,

Believe in faith

And you will become

Faithful.

FAREWELL FOR NOW

Farewell for now

But we won't say

goodbye,

Because if we said

goodbye

Forever

I think I would cry.

Farewell

for Now

I have to say,

It's a small world

We'll meet again.

If we don't,

I'll always remember

How good of a friend

You were of mine.

Time finally got

Its revenge on us

And I just want to say

That I'll miss you

So much.

It's good to have met you,

It's good to have known you.

I love to meet friends

I love to say hi,

But the worst thing I hate

Is saying goodbye.

So, let's just say

Farewell

for now

FEELINGS

The way you make me feel

I just can't explain,

The way you make me feel

Just rattles my brain.

When I am next to you

A feeling

Just runs down my spine,

I know

That if I lose you

I'll go

Out of

My mind.

That's why I try so hard

To please you

So much,

That's why I feel so good

Just by

The feeling of your touch.

You mean so much to me

I just can't

Fully

Explain,

It's the way you make me feel

That drives me insane.

I just had to say

That I love you

So,

And if you ever

Try to get away

from me,

It's because

of the way

You make me feel

I won't ever

Let you go.

FEELINGS OF LOVE

Feelings of love

Is what I feel

When I see you.

Feelings of love

Is what I feel

When I touch you.

Feeling of love

Is what I feel

When I am warm.

Inside

Feelings of love

Is what I feel

When I am close

To you.

Feelings of love

Is what I feel

When I am

Loving you.

FOR THOSE WHO KNEW ME

For those who knew me

They knew me well,

For those who knew me

They always seem to tell.

For those who knew me

They said it was a joy,

For those who knew me

They always seem to say

That I was a very good

Looking boy.

For those who knew me

They always seem to say

That it was a pleasure

To know me,

For those who knew me

They always seem to say

That I was very good company

When they were lonely.

For those who didn't

know me

I am sorry to say

That you

missed out,

Lucked out,

And wasted half

of your life away.

FRIENDS FOREVER

You've been with me

Through all the years,

Through happy days

And sad wet tears.

You've been with me

Through all the grief,

You've helped me out

With my problems

That I could not have reached.

We've been so close

We've been so near,

To share the happiness

Of those long years.

If I had a chance

To live again,

You would still

Be my number one friend.

You've taught me that life

Is much more than fun

As the days went by

One by one.

You and I

I and you,

No matter what goes first

The feeling of friendship

Will always

flow through...

Dedicated to My Best friend

My Ride or Die

my number one Brother,

Freddy Boy Woods.

GET YOUR HOUSE IN ORDER!

IF THE LORD

WAS COMING BACK

TOMORROW,

WOULD YOU

TRULY BE READY?

IF YOU KNEW

FOR SURE

THAT YOU

COULDN'T PRAY

ANYMORE

OR

ASK GOD

FOR MERCY

AND

FORGIVENESS

OR

REPENT

FOR YOUR SINS!

BECAUSE FOR YEARS

YOU'VE KNOWN

THAT GOD

HAS BEEN

FORGIVING YOU

AND SHOWING

YOU MERCY

FOR YOUR SINS,

FOR YEARS,

AND

HE CAN READ

YOUR HEART,

YOUR THOUGHTS,

YOUR EVERYTHING!

WOULD YOU BE READY?

TO BE

SPIRITUALLY CHANGED,

TO BE

WITH THE LORD!

OR

WOULD YOU

GO TO HELL

WITH THE DEVIL

AND

HIS FOLLOWERS?

THINK ABOUT IT!

WE KNOW NOT

THE HOUR

NOR

THE TIME!

BUT THE SIGNS

ARE HERE.

BIBLE VERSES:

Matthew 24:42 – "Therefore keep watch, because you do not know on what day your Lord will come"

Matthew 24:42-51– To watch for Christ's coming, is to maintain that temper of mind which we would be willing that our Lord should find us in. We know we have but a little time to live, we cannot know that we have a long time to live; much less do we know the time fixed for the judgment. Our Lord's coming will be happy to those that shall be found ready, but very dreadful to those that are not. If a man professing to be the servant of Christ, be an unbeliever, covetous, ambitious, or a lover of pleasure, he will be cut off. Those who choose the world for their portion in this life, will have hell for their portion in the other life. May our Lord, when he cometh, pronounce us blessed, and present us to the Father, washed in his blood, purified by his Spirit, and fit to be partakers of the inheritance of the saints in light...

Revelation 3:3–Remember, then, what you received and heard. Keep it, and repent. If you will not wake up, I will come like a thief, and you will not know at what hour I will come against you.

2 Peter 3:10–But the day of the Lord will come like a thief, and then the heavens will pass away with a roar and the heavenly bodies will be burned up and dissolved, and the earth and the works that are done on it will be exposed.

Romans 13:11–Besides this you know the time, that the hour has come for you to wake from sleep. For salvation is nearer to us now than when we first believed.

Luke 21:34–"But watch yourselves lest your hearts be weighed down with dissipation and drunkenness and cares of this life, and that day come upon you suddenly like a trap."

Revelation 2:5–Remember therefore from where you have fallen; repent, and do the works you did come to you and remove your lampstand from its place, unless you repent and do the works you did at first. If not I will come to you and remove your lampstand from its place unless you repent.

GIRLS ARE SEXY

Girls are sexy

Girls are sweet,

I love when girls

Get next to me.

They smell so sweet

They look divine,

Girls are lucky

They're so fine.

GOD SAID

GOD SAID!

YOU'LL BE

OKAY

YOU'LL BE

OKAY

GOD SAID

YOU'LL BE

OKAY

YOU'LL BE

OKAY

GOD SAID

YOU'LL BE

OKAY

NEVER

STOP

PRAISING HIM

NEVER

STOP

CALLING HIM

GET ON YOUR KNEES

AND BEG!

FOR MERCY,

FROM HIM!

SHED

YOUR TEARS

FOR HIM,

OPEN

YOUR HEART

TO HIM,

GIVE UP

YOUR LIFE

FOR HIM,

BE

AND

REMAIN

OBEDIENT

TO HIM,

CONFESS YOUR SINS
TO HIM

AND

ADORE HIM,

NEVER

STOP

WORSHIPING

HIM!

AND YOU'LL BE OK AND YOU'LL BE OK NEVER STOP LISTENING TO HIM NEVER STOP READING HIS WORD! NEVER STOP OBEYING HIM NEVER STOP CARING, NEVER ABANDONED HIM,

ALWAYS

WALK

WITH HIM!

ALWAYS

TRUST

IN HIM

NEVER

STOP

LOVING HIM!

NEVER!

AND

YOU'LL

BE OK

AND

YOU'LL BE OK.

GOD SENT ME AN ANGEL

SO, I PRAYED

TO GOD

ABOVE

FOR SOMEONE TO KEEP

FOR SOMEONE TO HOLD

FOR SOMEONE TO HUG

FOR SOMEONE TO LOVE

AND GOD

ANSWERED MY PRAYERS

AND

SENT ME

A WIFE

OF PURE GOLD,

FROM HEAVEN ABOVE,

YOU'RE ALL MY DREAMS

WRAPPED UP IN ONE!

THAT CAME TRUE

AND

THATS WHY

MY HEART

HAS THIS

LOVE AFFAIR

WITH NO ONE

BUT YOU

YOU WON

MY HEART

FROM DAY ONE

FROM THE MOMENT

I SEEN YOUR FACE

YOU TOOK

MY HEART

FROM ME

AND

IT NEVER ESCAPED

MY LOVE FOR YOU

IS PURE

AND

ALWAYS BEEN THE SAME

YOU DRIVE

MY MIND

AND

SOUL CRAZY!

AND

MY HEART

SURELY INSANE

YOU ARE

MY WIFE,

MY LOVE,

MY DEAR

HEART

AND

NOTHING

IN THIS WORLD

WOULD NEVER

EVER

SPLIT US APART!

YOUR PICTURE

IS IN MY ARMS

EVERY TIME

THAT I FALL

ASLEEP

AND

I GET A WARM

FEELING

OF YOUR LOVE

IN MY SOUL

IN MY HEART

AND EVEN

IN MY FEET

YOU'RE NEVER

APART FROM ME

BECAUSE

I AM WARMED

BY YOUR TOUCH!

AND

YOU'RE ALWAYS

LOCKED AWAY

IN MY HEART

WITH LOVE!

OH SO MUCH!

IF I HAVEN'T

SAID THESE THINGS

TO YOU

EVER BEFORE

MY DEAR WIFE

I LOVE YOU

ALWAYS

AND

FOREVER MORE.

If I NEVER TOLD YOU

I REALLY LOVE YOU

OR EXPRESSED

HOW

I REALLY FEEL!

IT'S MY HEART

THAT YEARNS FOR YOU!

AND

YOUR LOVE

THAT MAKES IT REAL!

YOU WILL NEVER

CRY FOR ME

OR

YOUR HEART

WILL NEVER FEEL LOW

BECAUSE

I WILL SPEND A LIFETIME

TELLING YOU

HOW MUCH

I LOVE

AND

CHERISH YOU SO,

AND I

WILL NEVER

EVER

LET YOU GO!

YOU ARE

MY LADY,

MY WIFE,

MY FRIEND,

MY LIFE,

AND

I WILL NEVER

STOP

LOVING YOU,

UNTIL MY END!

PEOPLE WILL QUESTION

IF MY LOVE

FOR YOU WAS REAL!

TELL THEM

WORDS CAN NOT EXPRESS

WHAT YOUR HEART

ALWAYS FEELS

SO SAY

NO WORDS,

JUST

GREET THEM

WITH A SMILE

AND

LET THEM KNOW

THAT THIS!

MY TRUE LOVE

WAS WORTH

ITS WHILE

NO ONE KNOWS

YOUR HEART

BUT

GOD ABOVE

AND

HE'S THE ONE

WHO BLESSED

THIS TRULY

UNITED LOVE.

GONE BUT NOT FORGOTTEN

An earth bound angel

Got her wings today,

She was earthbound

for many years

And now,

She's on her way.

She's an angel of beauty

Of purity and kindness,

She stood her ground

In faithfulness

And

She concord

Her trials and tribulations.

And GOD received her,

In his arms

And said to her

You did more

Than your best,

No more tears!

No more loneliness

No more hurting,

And

No more pain,

Because

Beneath my wings,

You shall rest,

And

Your soul

I shall

Surely

Sustain.

So, when you

Remember her,

Remember her laugh,

Remember her smiles,

Remember her prayers,

And do the same,

And if you

Cry!

Do not

Cry

For long!

Because it's through

Her strength

That you must,

Go on.

So, remember the good times

So, remember the joy

So, remember the fun,

And push on

In faithfulness,

Because GOD

And we all

Are one,

We are all testimonies

Until our own day

Is done.

So, remember

She was a friend

She comforted

And cared

For those who were close,

And

For those who needed her

She loved them,

The most.

Remember she was a wife

Committed,

Honest,

And true

Remember her promise

In your hearts

Is where

You will find her,

And she will never

Leave

Nor forsaken

You.

But, most of all

Remember

She was a mother

Who cradled and nurtured

Her children

Forever more,

And with anything

So precious

It was her children

That she adored.

So, let her sleep

Under the LORD'S

command,

And with an utter

Of his word

She will live again.

So,

Let's not say goodbye

So,

Let's not fuss

Nor fight,

But instead

Let's say farewell

Sweet angel

Rest in peace,

Goodnight...

HAVE I FOUND YOU

Oh, beautiful one

Where have you been?

My search

Was long

And hard

been

I even bowed down

To sin

You are so pretty

Are you free?

Please give me

A chance to see

If you are

The right one for me

I am tired now,

I want to forget the past

Have I found her

in you,

At last?

You smile so beautifully

You seem such a delight,

Are you

What I've seen in the distance

Or

Are you

that bright light?

Come close to me

Let me touch your face,

What a sensation

Is this the end

of my chase?

Tell me sweetheart

Will you be mine?

What should I look for?

What is my sign?

I'll treat you

Like a queen

I'll hold you

high,

Let's walk the road

Of love together

Let's aim

For the sky.

HAVE YOU EVER

Have you ever

Thought

in your mind

That you

would be

Left alone

one day

And

the person

in your heart

Would never

seem to say?

Have you ever

In your eyes

Seen the tears

that you shed,

For someone

you care about

so

And

the reason

Why

you're

Shedding these tears

Is because you're afraid

That the person

would soon

Let you go?

Have you ever

Felt the love

In your heart

Start to fade away

And you try to stop it

so

Because

only you know

That you want

that love

To grow

Not to go?

Have you ever

Felt warm

around that person

Because you shared

so much

Together

And then

it got cold

Because

you both knew

That it wasn't going to last

Forever?

Have you ever

Tried to talk

To that person

And knew that person

Didn't want to talk

To you,

And there was nothing

You could do?

Have you ever

Tried to speak

To that person

To make that person

see,

Have you ever

Tried to tell that person

That I know it's hurting you

But it's also hurting me?

Have you ever

Been truly in love

With that person

And you both said

That you

would never

Depart,

Have you ever

Been truthful

And now to know

That person

Has broken your

Heart?

I have.

HELL BEGINS

A beast was thrown

Into a fiery zone

To be condemned

To be alone

To make that fiery zone

His home

He was cast down below

with a fire so steep

The devil we are told

In hell was chained

And a thousand years

He there remained

He never complained

Nor did he grown

But determined to start

A hell of his own

Where he could torment

The souls of sinful men

And that is how

Hell began.

HOW

How

Am I

To start over

Knowing

It's not you

I am

Starting

Over

With?

How

am I

to start over

Knowing

So much

Of you

I'll surely

Miss?

How

Am I

To start over

With

Someone

New?

How

Am I

To start over

When

I am still

In love

With you?

HOW BEAUTIFUL OUR GOD IS

We can feel

The touch

of

His hands,

Through the wind,

We can see

The warmth

of

His smile,

On Our face,

Through the sun,

We can see

The twinkle

In

His eyes

Through the stars,

We can see

His love

and

compassion,

That He has,

For us.

Through the rain,

Of

His tears,

What a wonderful

GOD

We

have

up

above,

Full

of

grace,

Full

of

compassion,

Full

of

mercy,

Full

of

love,

How

beautiful,

our

GOD

Is

To us.

Dedicated to the one and only,

GOD above...

HOW BEAUTIFUL YOU ARE TO ME

Before

I close my eyes

I look upon your face,

I look upon your structure

Your beauty

And grace.

I Look upon your smile

That's spread across

Your cheeks,

Without a question

Is to why

My heart

Gets so weak.

Could it be

Your style

Your pizazz

Or

Your elegant ways,

That makes my mind

Ponder

About your love

Each

And

Everyday.

HOW MANY HEARTACHES

How many heartaches

Do we have to take?

How

many heartaches

Do we have to break?

So many times,

We've been heartbroken

In two,

And we're confused

And don't know

What to do.

We sit and cry

All night long,

And wonder why

Things always seem

To go wrong.

How many hearts

Do we have to search?

How

many miles

Do we have to run

To get to the one

That

We always love

First?

Love seems

So hard

But we seem

To play the game,

Over and over again,

And it always

Seems to lead up

To the same old thing

That we never can't

Seem to take

Heartaches,

Because we always,

Seem to get

Our feelings hurt,

How many chances

Do we have to take,

How many tries

Do we get?

How

many times

Do we have to give up,

If finding someone

Special

Never seems,

To work?

I AM FALLING IN LOVE

I am falling in love

And I

just want to show it,

I am falling in love

And I

just want you

to know it.

I am falling in love

And

there's nothing

In this world

That you can do

Except say

That you're happy

That

I am falling in love

With you,

And hope

That

You're very much

In love

With me too.

I am falling In love

And I'll make you mine,

I am falling in love

And it took

So much time.

But it was worth

Every moment

Because

I am falling in love

With no one

but you.

Out of all of things

That I want you

To know,

Just remember

One thing

That

I will always

Love you so.

I AM FOREVER IN LOVE WITH YOU

I am forever,

In love with you,

There's nothing

In the world

I'd rather do,

Then give my heart

And love to you.

You're everything

That I have ever

Dreamt of,

In the dictionary

Your name

Is above the word

Love.

You're my heart

You're my soul

And

I just

want you to know,

That I will

Never

Ever

Let you

Go.

I AM GOING TO MISS YOU

I am going to miss

The things we did

And the things we seen

I am going to miss you

Because forever more

You mean to me

I am going to miss

Being with you

In every moment

of the day

I am going to miss

The times we spent

Walking in the rain

I am going to miss

Those thoughtful things

You did for me

And those sensitive words

You use to say

I am going to miss

Your loving face

And your sweet

Shinning smile

I am going to miss

The things we had

Because to me

They were worthwhile

I am going to miss

Your warm caresses

Your soft kisses

And all

Your loving ways

I am going to miss

You

Everyday

I am going to miss

The tears we shed

Together

And the laughter

I am going to miss

you

Today,

Always,

and

Forever

After.

I AM ME

I am a person

I shall be free

Who am I

I am me

I shall run wild

I shall be free

Who am I

I am me

I may not be rich

But I am not poor

I may not have a lock

But I may have a door

What can I do

What shall I be

Who am I

I am me.

I AM SO DEPRESSED WITHOUT YOU

I am so depressed

I have worries on my chest

I am so depressed

And I don't know what to do

Because I am so lonely

Without you

I am so depressed

Every time that I see you

I just walk away

Because I don't know

What to do,

Because I don't know

What to say,

I am so depressed

Because I am afraid

That you might say

Where breaking apart

And if you do

Say these words

You'll be breaking

My heart

I am so depressed

I can't walk

With my head high

Because

Every time I think of you

I always start

To cry,

I am so depressed

I remember the days

That we had our share

I remember the time

That I whispered

In your ear

And told you

That I love you

And I will always

Be there,

I remember the time

That you cared for me so

I remember the time

That you said

You would never

Let me go

I am so depressed

Because I have worries

On my mind

And tears in my eyes

Because I have visions

Of you

Saying goodbye.

I AM SO LONELY

You are my heart

And I feel so

Lonely without you,

I need you, baby,

Your papi needs you

So much

I miss you

So much

I can't stand,

Being away from you

Any longer!

My heart cries

For you

Everyday!

Baby,

I miss you,

I am so sad

Sometimes

I miss you,

I want to be

In your arms,

I want you

To kiss me,

To hold me

Tight!

tell me,

That you

love me,

that's what I need,

Baby!

I need you,

I just want

To hold you

For as long

As it takes

Me to breathe again.

I AM SO LONELY WITHOUT YOU

I am so lonely without you

Just the thought of you

Makes my tears

Start to roll down

My eyes,

And the more I think

About you

The more I start to cry.

It is you

Who I want to hold

Every moment of the day,

I am so lonely without you

every time you go away.

I get pains in my head

When I think of you

So much,

I get pains everywhere

When I remember

The feeling of your touch.

Every time that I am away

From you

I feel something isn't right,

Because every time

I go to sleep

I see visions of you

In my dreams at night.

I am so lonely without you

every time

I take out

your picture

I give it

just one kiss,

And

every time

I think of others

It is you

That I

Surely miss.

I always start to cheer

Myself up

By doing

Something else

By then,

my mind wonders

And

I think of you

again

And then

my heart

Begins to melt.

I am so lonely without you

I feel we're running out of time,

I can't eat

Nor can I sleep

Because you're always

On my

mind.

WHERE I AM FROM

Where I am from

Mothers are crying

because

their children

are dying,

because now

they're sprouting

Out wickedness

in their songs

of rhyming,

they can't leave

these streets

alone,

now there's

one dead,

And

the gun goes

pop pop

dat dat

Now I am back

on your block

to continue

the Bloodshed

now, the killer's dead,

Yet!

Another one

shot in the head

because of

beef

speaks,

of disrespect

in these streets,

it's time!

to grab

and get

the heat,

with

100 rounds

in the Ak 47,

time to gather up

my homies,

time to get

my crew!

Time to ride

through these
boroughs
time to clear
these streets
and end
all the beef,
it's time!
To do
what AKs
and bullets
were made
to do!
Get ready
Sweep!
It's time
to do
what it do!
Now the night
is done,
dropped many
not just one!
Mothers crying,
my opps

are dying!

Projectiles drooping

bullets flying!

And as

the sun

come up,

the streets

get quiet,

No talking

No snitching!

No one

gives a Fuck!

I hear

police sirens,

and mothers

screaming

for their children,

their hearts broke 💔

and

their words

of

aching tears

and

silent crying! ☹

Where I am from

the people

are proud,

the music

is loud,

even the bums

go through

the trash

just to eat,

On these streets!

the people

are fast

everything

is always

a hustle

just to earn

to make

or get

to take

that cash!

You see

in my town,

you can't

be a wimp

or a small time

sucker!

You got to be

born here,

you got to be

made here!

Not a punk!

You got to be

like no other,

you got to be

brave and strong!

Running through

these mean streets

with Authority!

Not someone soft!

that melts,

like

butter

You see

Where I am from

you can have it

your way,

whatever you want,

whenever you need it!

You have to go

get it!

By any means

Is

necessary

With a gun,

with a knife 🔪

Even

with a beat down

Or

an Olde fashion

Fist fight,

That's our commentary

Bring it!

We'll leave you

laid out

Or dead

in these streets,

and if you live,

well

We Will

be waiting

for you!

Did you guess?

Do you know?

I'll tell you,

We're ruthless!

And I am

A

New Yorker

And

we never sleep!

OUR LOVE

OUR LOVE

IS A GODLY LOVE

THAT WILL LAST

FOREVER

FROM THE START,

GUIDED BY GOD

AND

EQUALLY YOKED

FROM THE HEART.

FROM THE FIRST

MOMENT

THAT I SAW YOU

I KNEW

THAT YOU WERE

THE ONE FOR ME,

I ASKED GOD

FOR

CONFORMATION

AND

HE SAID YES

THAT

YOUR HEART

AND

MY HEART

ARE

JOINED

TOGETHER

AND

MEANT

TO BE.

THEN, I KNEW

THAT I WAS

TRULY BLESSED!

GOD

DID NOT

GIVE ME

AVERAGE,

GOD

DID NOT

GIVE ME

ORDINARY,

HE GAVE ME

EXQUISITELY

THE BEST!

YOU ARE

ONE OF A KIND

PICKED FROM GOD ABOVE,

TOGETHER FOREVER

SHARING GOD'S

SPIRITUAL LOVE.

I'LL ALWAYS

WANT YOU

TILL

THE END

OF TIME,

BECAUSE GOD

HAS GIVEN US

A STAMP OF APPROVAL

FROM HEAVEN

FOR ALL TIMES

HE MADE YOU

MINE.

I HAVE

BEEN WAITING

FOR YOU

FOREVER

I WAS EVEN

FOOLED
WHEN LOVE CAME
AROUND,
BUT
I HAD TO REALIZE
THAT
TRUE LOVE
HAS TO BE
GODLY SENT
NOT WORLDLY
OR
EARTHLY BOUND.
SO, TRUST
IN GOD
IN ALL
THAT
YOU DO,
AND
CONTINUE
TO WALK
BY FAITH
AND
ALWAYS KNOW

THAT GOD

HAS CREATED

MY HEART

FOR

NO ONE

BUT YOU.

OUR BLACKNESS

IS BEAUTIFUL

AND

POWERFUL!

FACE DOWN

ON THE GROUND

IS WHERE

YOU WANT US!

WITH OUR HANDS

CUFFED

BEHIND OUR BACKS!

BUT YOU STILL

SHOOT

AND

CONTINUE

TO DESTROY US!

WITH SEVERAL BULLETS

IN OUR BACKS!

WE KNOW

THE TRUE FACTS!

IT'S BECAUSE

WE'RE BLACK!

YOU SAY

WE'RE RESISTING ARREST

EVEN

WITH A CHOKEHOLD

SUBMISSION

AND

YOUR KNEE,

PUSHED

AND

PRESSED DOWN!

AGAINST OUR CHEST

YOU SAY

WE DON'T COMPLY!

BUT

WE'RE NOT READY

TO DIE!

THAT'S WHY!

WHEN YOU MAKE

YOUR VERBAL COMMANDS

AND

DIRECT THREATS

WITH ONE HAND

ON YOUR GUN

AND

THE OTHER

ON OUR BEAUTIFUL

BLACK NECKS!

BEFORE

WE ARE GIVEN A CHANCE

TO ADVANCE

TO YOUR DEMANDS!

OUR BLACK BODIES

ARE

BEAT,

STRANGLED,

STOMPED,

MURDERED,

AND SHOT!

BY

YOUR

GUILTY,

DIRTY,

FILTHY,

WHITE,

RACIST

POLICEMEN

HANDS!

IS IT SOMETHING

WE SAID

THAT WE

JUST

CAN'T

TAKE BACK?

OR IS IT TRULY

THE COLOR OF

OUR SKIN!

OR IS IT

THE RICHNESS,

THE BEAUTY,

THE BLACKNESS,

THE TRUE

AND

LIVING

ELOHIM!

THAT SHINES

WITHIN US

THAT YOU

JUST

CAN'T STAND!

DEDICATED TO MY FALLEN BROTHERS

BY THE WHITE POLICEMEN.

A PLAN TO ERADICATE THE BLACK RACE

JUSTIFICATION

OF FALSE

EMANCIPATION

WITH DELIBERATE

MANIPULATION

TO SEE

TODAY

OUR WALKING

PAPERS,

TO GEAR

THIS SYSTEMATIC

SYSTEM

OF WHITE

SUPREMACY

THE SKINHEADS

THE NEO NAZI'S

THE KKK

THE WHITE MAN,

THE WHITE RACE,

ESAU

THE EUROPEANS

AS IT BE

FROM THE ELITES

TO THE MASSES

A CONFIRMATION

TO AGREE

IS SET

BY A MASSIVE

INDUCEMENT,

OF REINCARNATING

OUR HISTORY

OF

MURDER

MISEDUCATION

AND

INCARCERATION

TO SET UPON

OUR PEOPLE

THE DARK RACE,

THE BLACKS

THE NEGROS

THE COLOREDS

THE AFRICAN

AMERICANS,

JUDAH

THE ISRAELITES

AS WE BE

AS A DESTRUCTION

AND

AN EMOTIONAL TURMOIL

OF OUR CULTURAL

SPIRITUAL

ECONOMICAL

CIVILIZATION

AND

SOCIALISM

IN SOCIETY.

ALL I EVER WANTED

I remember

that heartache

That heartbreak

That pain

That would never seem to go away,

And the tears that I shed so much

Because I wanted you to stay.

I thought that my life was over!

And it seemed that way,

at that very moment,

for sure!

It was the end,

and my life

Was doomed

Towards torment.

Because loving you

forever

Is all

I ever

wanted to do.

If love was something

I was supposed to learn

through life lessons,

I've learnt nothing!

Because my life

was only you,

You're all

I ever wanted,

You're all

I ever wanted

It to be.

I never

ever

wanted

To say goodbye

But I guess

I have no choice now

That you left me.

The days

The months

The years

Are slower

Now

That

The beat of my heart,

is in agony!

Why is my heart

beating so painfully

Was there something

I have done in my life,

so cruel-fully

that I deserve this

From you?

For what

you've done

to me,

I just wanted love

In my life!

That's all I've ever

Wanted for me!

But now

All I have

Is my

Heartache drowning

in

Pain,

Sorrow,

And

Misery

There's no more

seconds

nor minutes

nor days

Or

tomorrows,

For me

Now

that you've gone

and

left me.

Made in United States
Orlando, FL
23 December 2023